HIDING IN
MOUNTAINS

Deborah Underwood

Heinemann Library
Chicago, Illinois

www.capstonepub.com
Visit our website to find out more information about Heinemann-Raintree books.

To order:
☎ Phone 800-747-4992
💻 Visit www.capstonepub.com
to browse our catalog and order online.

© 2011 Heinemann Library
an imprint of Capstone Global Library, LLC
Chicago, Illinois

Edited by Rebecca Rissman and Nancy Dickmann
Designed by Joanna Hinton Malivoire
Picture research by Tracy Cummins
Originated by Capstone Global Library
Printed and bound in the United States of America in North Mankato, Minnesota. 062013 007580RP

15 14 13
10 9 8 7 6 5 4 3

Library of Congress Cataloging-in-Publication Data
Underwood, Deborah.
  Hiding in mountains / Deborah Underwood. -- 1st ed.
    p. cm. -- (Creature camouflage)
  Includes bibliographical references and index.
  ISBN 978-1-4329-4023-2 (hc) -- ISBN 978-1-4329-4032-4 (pb) 1. Mountain animals--Juvenile literature. 2. Camouflage (Biology)--Juvenile literature. I. Title.
  QL113.U53 2010
  591.47'2--dc22
                              2009051766

Acknowledgments
The author and publisher are grateful to the following for permission to reproduce copyright material:
Getty Images pp. 23, 24 (Michael S. Quinton), 28 (Richard Ellis); istockphoto pp. 4 (© John Woodworth); National Geographic Stock pp. 11, 12 (Norbert Rosing); Photo Researchers, Inc. pp. 15, 16 (Dante Fenolio); Photolibrary pp. 6 (View Stock), 8 (Anton Luhr), 9 (James Urbach), 10 (Tom Ulrich); Photoshot pp. 17, 18, 21, 22 (© NHPA); Shutterstock pp. 5 (© Vaclav Volrab), 7 (© Prono Filippo), 13, 14 (© René Baumgartner), 19, 20 (© Hiroyuki Saita), 29 (© david vadala); Visuals Unlimited Inc. pp. 25, 26 (© Thomas Marent), 27 (© Ashley Cooper).

Cover photograph of a snow leopard (Panthera uncia) reproduced with permission of Naturepl.com (© Francois Savigny).

We would like to thank Michael Bright for his invaluable help in the preparation of this book.

Contents

Some words are printed in bold, **like this**. You can find out what they mean by looking in the glossary.

What Are Mountains Like?

A mountain is an area of high land. Mountains can be found in most parts of the world. A group of mountains in one place is called a **mountain range**.

Many different plants and animals live on mountains.

Air gets cooler as you go higher up a mountain. Different parts of a mountain may have different **climates**. It may be hot at the bottom, but cold and snowy at the top.

Living in the Mountains

Many different animals live in mountain areas. Some live on cold, snowy mountaintops. Some live in rocky parts of desert mountains. Others live in mountain forests.

Giant pandas live in bamboo forests in the mountains of China.

A mountain goat's adaptations include special hooves and warm fur.

Some mountain animals have special **features** to help them **survive**. These features are called **adaptations**. For example, mountain goats have special hooves that keep them from slipping on rocks.

What Is Camouflage?

Camouflage (KAM-uh-flaj) is an **adaptation** that helps animals hide. The color of an animal's skin, fur, or feathers may match the things around it. Why do you think animals need to hide?

Skylarks make nests on the ground. Their feathers act as camouflage.

It is hard to see a snow leopard on a rocky slope!

An animal that eats other animals is called a **predator**. Predators often sneak up on the animals they are hunting. Camouflage helps predators hide as they hunt.

Bighorn sheep have fur that blends in with their surroundings.

Animals that **predators** eat are called **prey** animals. **Camouflage** helps prey animals **survive**, too. It allows them to **blend in** so predators can't spot them.

Find the Mountain Animals

Mountain lion

Mountain lions hunt by sneaking up on their prey. Their fur is the same color as the rocks and ground. This helps them to hide while they hunt.

CAMOUFLAGED

Sometimes a mountain lion kills a large animal. The lion eats some. Then it covers the rest of the animal with leaves or dirt. The lion comes back to eat more for several days.

REVEALED

Alpine marmot

Alpine marmots (AL-pine MAHR-muhts) are part of the squirrel family. Their fur is a mix of colors. This helps to **camouflage** them from **predators**, such as eagles and foxes.

Alpine marmots live in family groups. One marmot watches for danger. If the marmot sees a **predator**, it whistles a warning!

Japanese giant salamander

Japanese giant salamanders (SAL-uh-man-durs) live in cold mountain streams. They have bumpy brown and black skin. Their skin looks like the mud and rocks in the water.

CAMOUFLAGED

Japanese giant salamanders hunt for insects, fish, and crab. They can go for weeks without eating. They can grow to be almost five feet long!

REVEALED

Western rattlesnake

Western rattlesnakes hunt small animals, such as mice and rats. They have dark spots on their backs. Can you see how the spots help them hide while they hunt?

A rattlesnake has a **venomous** bite.
It shakes the rattle on its tail if danger
comes near. The rattling sound warns
predators to stay away.

Jackson's chameleon

Jackson's chameleons (kuh-MEE-lee-uhnz) live in trees. Their green color makes them hard to spot in the leaves. Chameleons may change color when they are excited or scared.

CAMOUFLAGED

A Jackson's chameleon sits very still when it hunts. Its **camouflage** helps it to hide. When an insect passes, the chameleon flicks out its tongue and catches a meal.

REVEALED

Mountain hare

Mountain hares eat plants. This means they must move around to look for food. The color of their coats helps them to hide from **predators**.

The mountain hare changes the color of its coat with the **seasons**. In summer its coat is brown. In winter it grows a white coat to match the snow.

REVEALED

Boreal owl

Boreal (BOR-ee-uhl) owls live in mountain pine forests. Their brown and white feathers **blend in** with the trees. This makes it harder for **predators** to spot them.

A boreal owl's **camouflage** also helps it hunt. It sits on a branch and listens carefully for **prey** passing below. When it hears a small animal or bird, the owl swoops down and catches it.

REVEALED

Lichen katydid

In Costa Rica, plantlike lichens (LIE-kuhns) grow in mountain forests. The lichen katydid (KAY-tee-dihd) **blends in** perfectly with the stringy lichen.

The lichen katydid's color helps it hide. So does its shape. Can you see how the spikes on the katydid's body make it even harder to see?

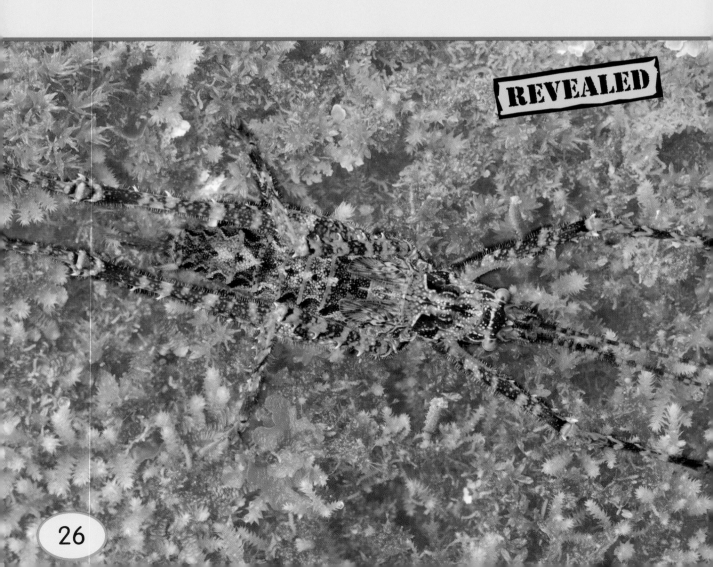

REVEALED

Even bird eggs can have camouflage!

Camouflage helps many mountain animals **survive**. If you are ever in the mountains, look closely. A camouflaged animal may be hiding nearby!

Animals that Stand Out

Many monarch (MAWN-ark) butterflies spend the winter in Mexican mountains. They hide when they rest. But when they fly, their bright wings stand out!

When monarch butterflies rest on trees, they look like dead leaves.

A monarch butterfly's bright colors tell **predators** to stay away.

Why don't monarch butterflies need to hide when they fly? Monarchs have **poisonous** bodies. Animals can get sick if they eat the butterflies. The bright color warns animals not to eat them!

Glossary

adaptation special feature that helps an animal survive in its surroundings

blend in matches well with the things around it

camouflage adaptation that helps an animal blend in

climate the usual weather in a place

feature special part of an animal

mountain range group of mountains

poisonous something dangerous that can make you sick, or even kill you, if eaten

predator animal that eats other animals

prey animal that other animals eat

seasons parts of the year that have different weather, such as spring, summer, fall, winter

survive stay alive

venomous something dangerous that can make you sick, or even kill you, if injected

Find Out More

Books to read

de Lambilly-Bresson, Elisabeth. *Animals of the Mountains*. Strongsville, OH: Gareth Stevens, 2007.

Gordon, Sharon. *Mountain Animals*. Tarrytown, NY: Benchmark Books, 2008.

Website

www.mountain.org/education/index.html
Learn about mountains from the Mountain Institute.

Index